# FRANCES
## the Fairy Dressmaker

by Susan Markowitz Meredith

illustrated by Jessica Wolk-Stanley

The sign in the window read, "Wand-Made Clothes Just For You!"

Inside, the fairy dressmaker's shop was very busy. The Prince's ball was that night. Ladies from across the kingdom were coming in for gowns.

Lady Abigail needed a new gown for the ball.

"Step over here, Lady Abigail," said Vivian, the fairy dressmaker.

Then Vivian asked her helper, Frances, to join them.

"Let's start," Vivian told Frances, "by looking at how Lady Abigail likes to dress."

Frances noticed that everything Lady Abigail wore looked the same on both sides. All of the bows looked the same. The buttons and pleats did, too. Even her hair was parted down the middle, with a bow on each side.

"Lady Abigail sure likes symmetry," said Frances.

"You're right," replied Vivian. "Now, let's match that symmetrical style with some natural objects."

Frances brought out their favorite book, "The Fairy's Book of Nature." She helped Vivian search through it, page by page.

birch

"These will do nicely," Vivian said. She pointed to pictures of a white begonia and a birch leaf.

"I'll get them right away," said Frances.

Vivian was happy to have such a good helper.

begonia

Frances hurried along the street, past the other shops.

At the edge of the kingdom was a garden Frances had visited many times.

"What a lovely flower," thought Frances, as she picked a white begonia. It had two small petals, on opposite sides, which looked exactly alike. Its two large petals were also the same.

"This looks symmetrical to me," she said. "It's a perfect match for Lady Abigail."

Suddenly, a bird flew past Frances.
It landed on a leafy branch. Frances knew
what those leaves were.

"That bird's in a birch tree!" she exclaimed.
This was just what she was looking for.

Frances found a low branch and picked
two birch leaves. She saw that each leaf was
divided into two halves. Each half had
the same shape.

"They're symmetrical, all right," she thought.

Frances looked at the bird again as it flew
from the birch tree. She smiled at the bird's
flapping wings. They were symmetrical, too.

When Frances got back to the shop, she was eager to watch Vivian transform the flower and leaves with her wand.

But Vivian had another idea. "Why don't you make the dress?" she asked Frances.

"Me?" replied Frances. She wasn't sure. She was still new at making dresses.

"You'll do fine," said Vivian.

Frances gave it a try. Slowly she lifted her wand and tapped the begonia, just the way Vivian had taught her.

To her delight, the white flower changed into a beautiful gown. Both sides of the gown looked exactly alike.

The slippers were next.

With a quick tap, Vivian turned the green birch leaves to bright yellow. That was their autumn color.

"Frances, why don't you take it from here?" Vivian suggested.

This time, Frances felt sure of herself.

She tapped the two leaves with her wand, and a pair of bright yellow slippers appeared.

Vivian thought they looked lovely.

But Lady Abigail's outfit still needed something. Vivian was sure of it.

The fruit bowl on the table gave her an idea. She took a lemon for herself and handed Frances an orange.

"Let's make a necklace," Vivian said.

Frances noticed that when she split the orange in two, both halves looked alike.

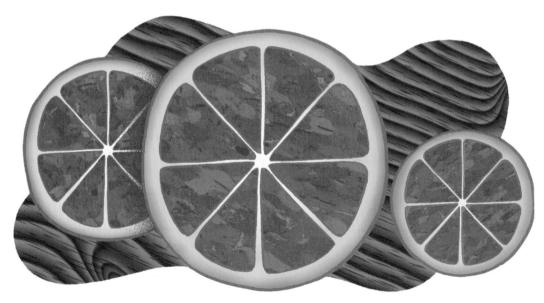

"Now that's symmetry," she declared.

"Just like this," replied Vivian, as she held up a round slice of lemon.

Frances and Vivian arranged the fruit in a circle. With the touch of a wand, the fruit became a beautiful necklace.

Lady Abigail's outfit was complete.

Lady Abigail returned to the shop to see her new gown.

"Why don't you try it on?" Vivian suggested. Lady Abigail was happy to do so.

Vivian's wand gently tapped the slippers, gown, and necklace. The next moment, Lady Abigail was wearing them.

"How beautiful and orderly," she said, looking at herself in the mirror.

Vivian and Frances smiled at each other. They had fit Lady Abigail's symmetrical style perfectly.

After Lady Abigail left, Vivian made a plate of sliced apples. "Great," said Frances. "It's a symmetrical snack."

"It fits the rest of our day," Vivian replied with a chuckle. As they sat and ate their apples, Vivian told Frances she was becoming a fine fairy dressmaker. Those words were as sweet to Frances as any fruit she'd ever tasted.